Athleticum

An art folio by

Alastair Wildfire

Dedicated to athletes and sportspersons everywhere. Your love for and passionate pursuit of skill and physical prowess will always inspire me.

Play fair, stay hydrated, do your best, and don't forget to have fun.

TABLE OF CONTENTS

GREYSCALE IMAGES -

Cyclying - Australian Cattle Dog   1
Para Powerlifting - Cougar/Coyote Hybrid   2
Tennis - Swift Fox   3
Parkour - Hare   4
Basketball - Red Squirrel   5
Japanese Archery - Kiso   6
Bodybuilding - African Civet   7
Baseball - Dingo   8
Swimming - Shark   9
Fishing - Gnoll   10
Soccer - Ring-tailed Lemur   11
Basketball - Crocodile   12
Bodybuilding - Flying Fox   13
Ballet - Borzoi   14
Knife-throwing - Irish Wolfhound   15
Wheelchair Basketball - Opossum   16
Yoga - Caracal   17
Hockey - Canadian Lynx   18
Basketball - Raccoon Dog   19
Pommel Horse - Siberian Tiger   20
Javelin - Caribou   21
Basketball - Magpie   22
Distance Running - Oryx   23
Tire Lift - Polar Bear   24
Beach Volleyball - Kangaroos   25
Vert Skateboarding - Maned Wolf   26
Pole-dancing - Tanuki   27
Fashion Model - Hare   28
Calisthenics - Smiloden   29
Longbow Archery - Fusky   30
Sailing - Thylacine   31
Fishing - Bloodhound   32
Motorcross - Cheetah   33-34

Boxing - Newt   35
Equestrian - Appaloosa   36
Bodybuilding - Eurasian Lynx   37
Dumbbell Rows - Mongoose   38
Pole-dancing - Asian Palm Civet   39
Caper Toss - Highland Cow   40
Surfing - Australian Shepherd   41
Weight-lifting - Doberman and Coyote   42
Hurdles - Baboon   43
Billiards - Mountain Lion   44
Weight-lifting - Kangaroo   45
Rope Toss - Bighorn Sheep   46
Free Climbing - Golden Retreiver   47
Planks - Australian Cattle Dog   48
Bodybuilding - Rhino   49
Lifeguard - Otter   50
Skiing - St. Bernard   51
Swimming - Otter   52
Kickboxing - Rhino   53
Billiards - Hyrax   54
Martial Arts - Kangaroo   55
Bodybuilding - Walrus   56

COLOR IMAGES -

Sailing - Thylacine   59
Lifeguard - Otter   60
Fashion Model - Hare   61
Vert Skateboarding - Maned Wolf   62
Free Climbing - Golden Retreiver   63
Billiards - Mountain Lion   64
Ballet - Boizoi   65

About the Artist/Publisher   67

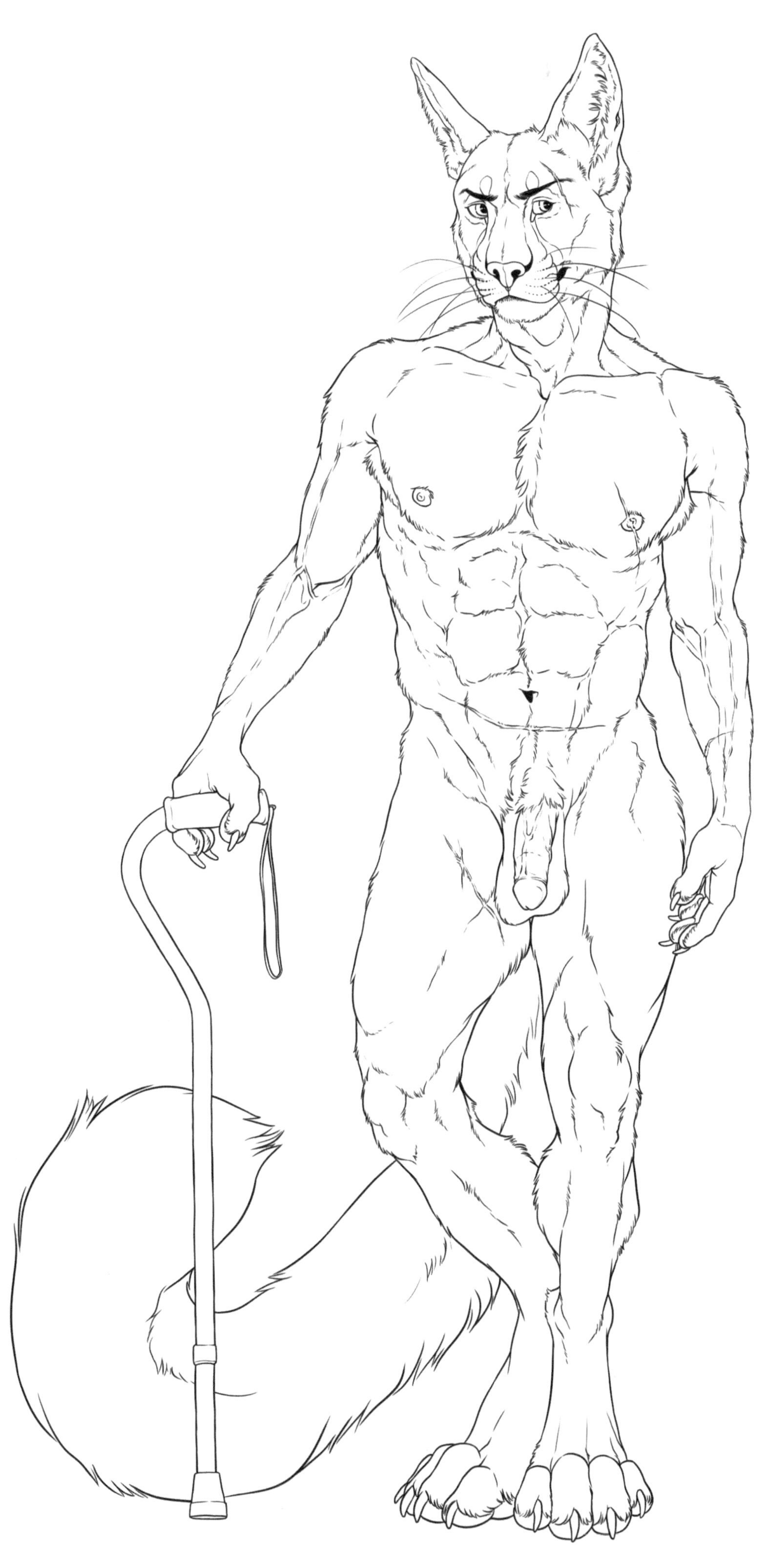

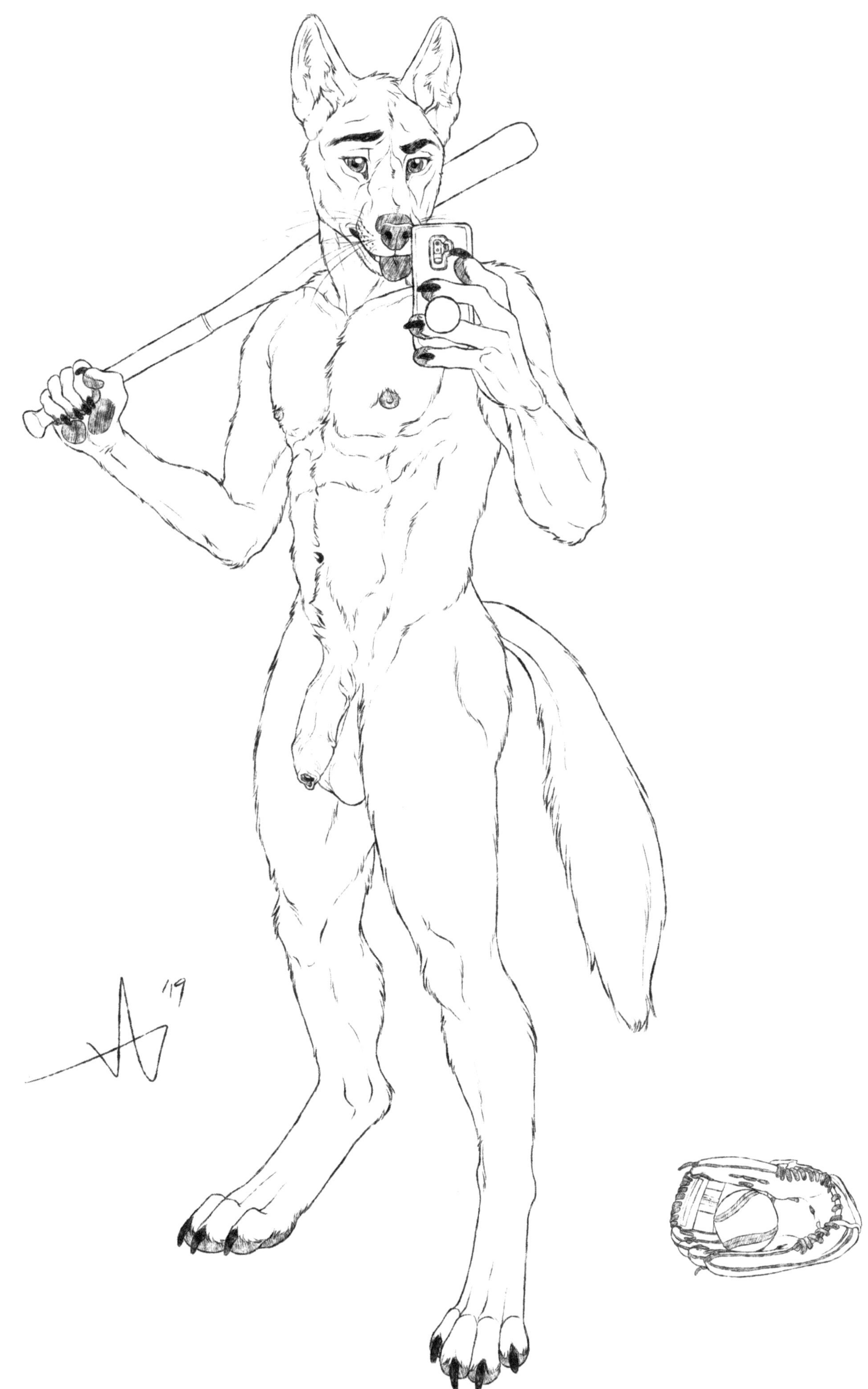

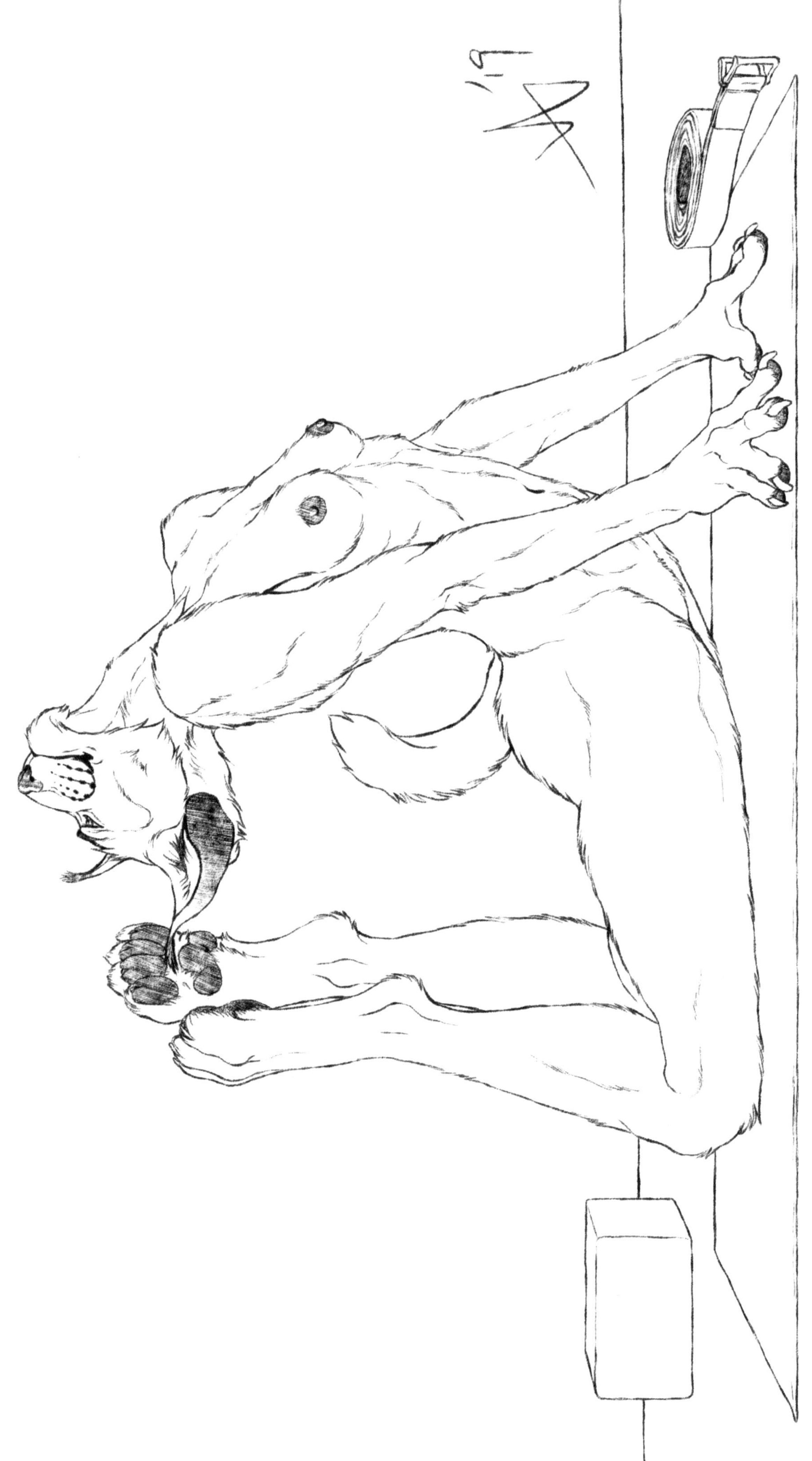

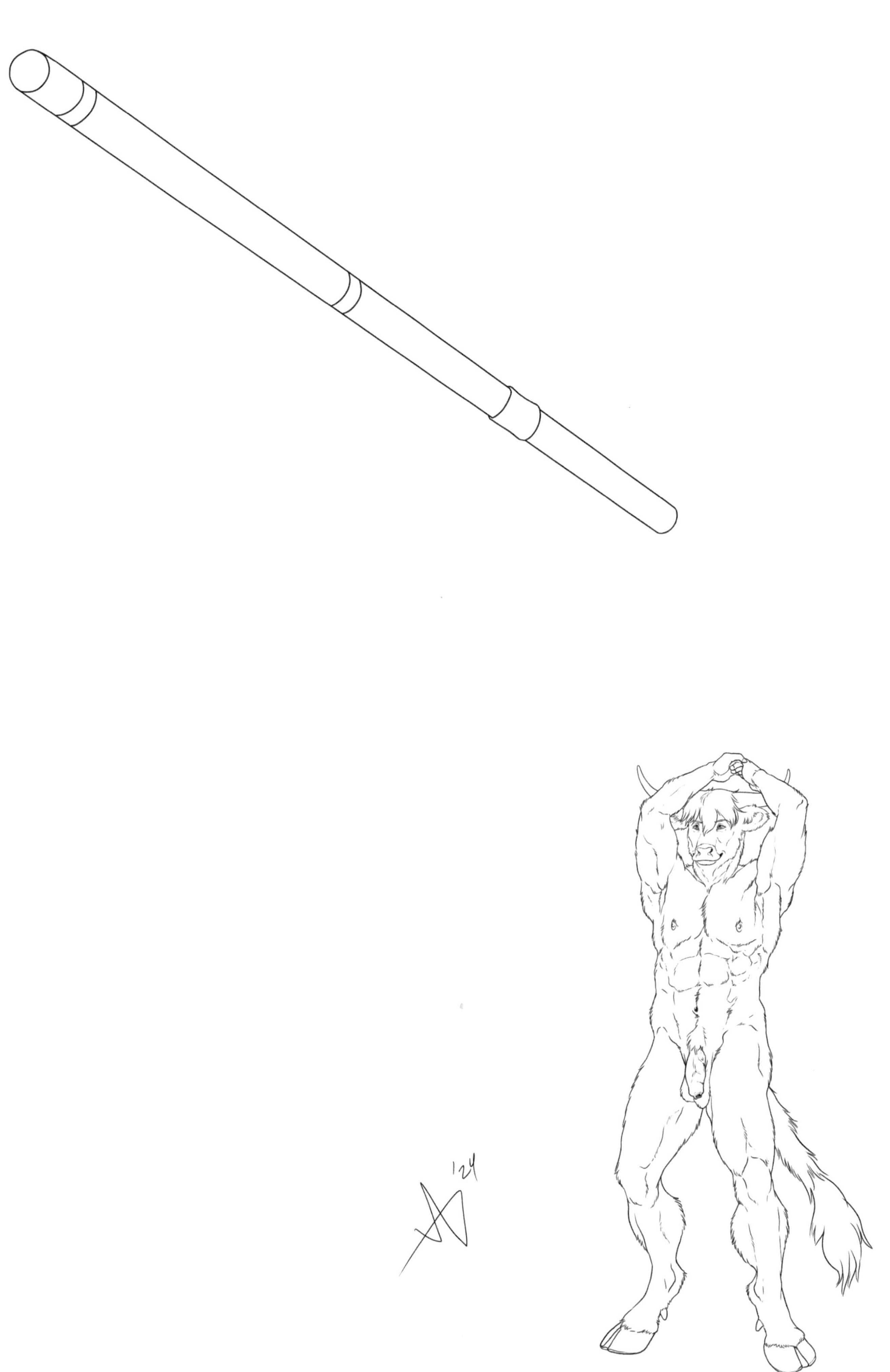

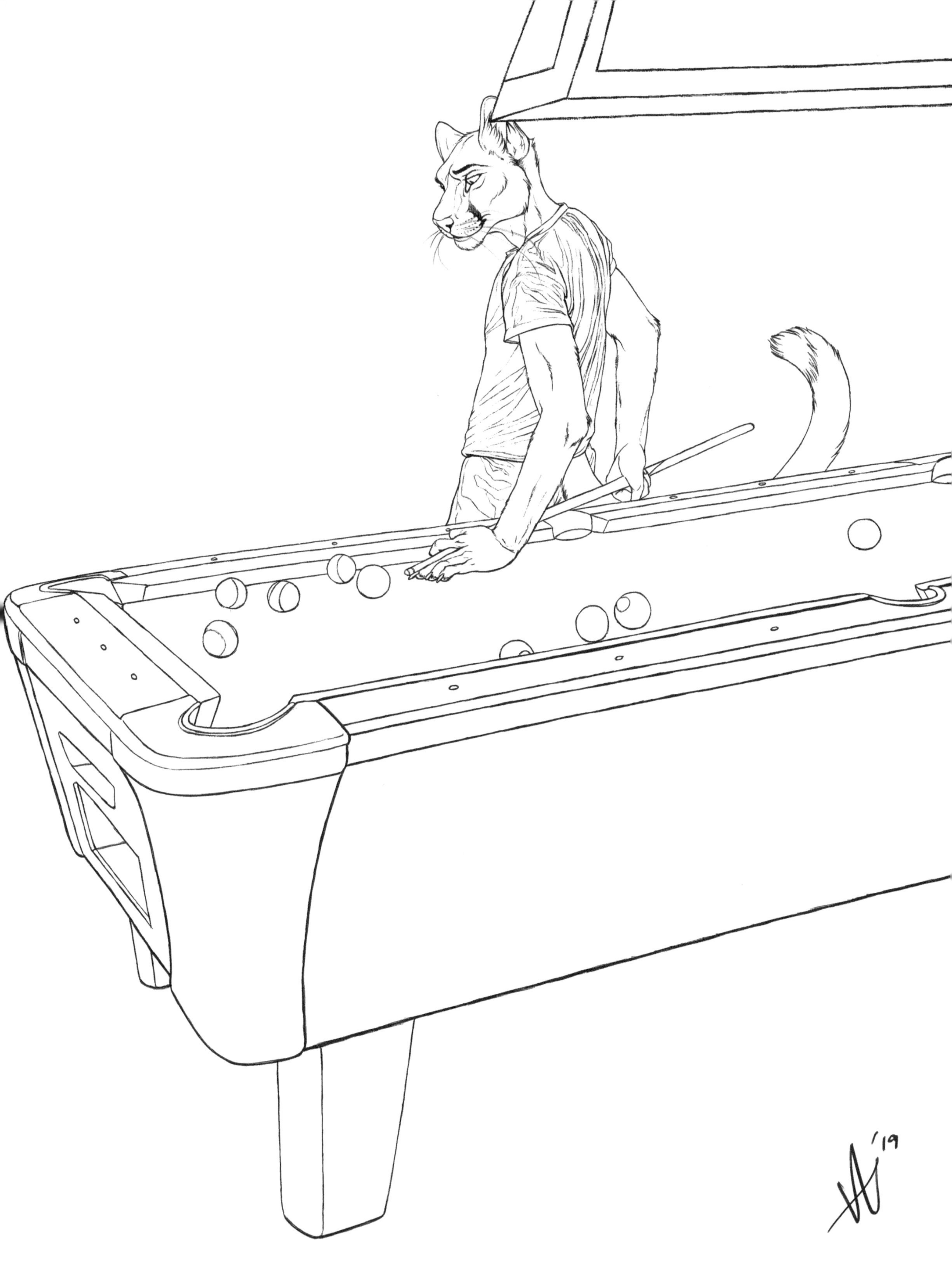

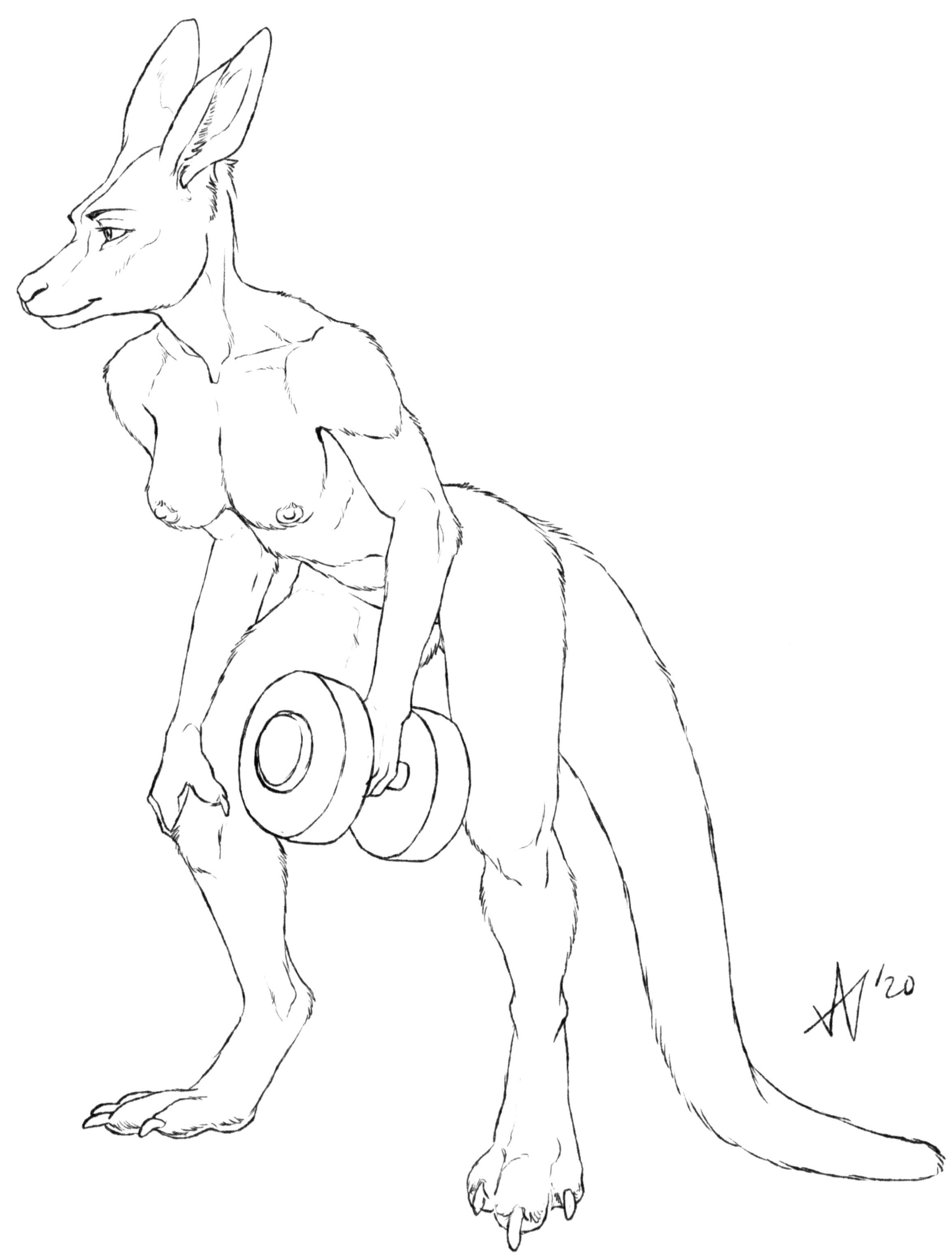

'24

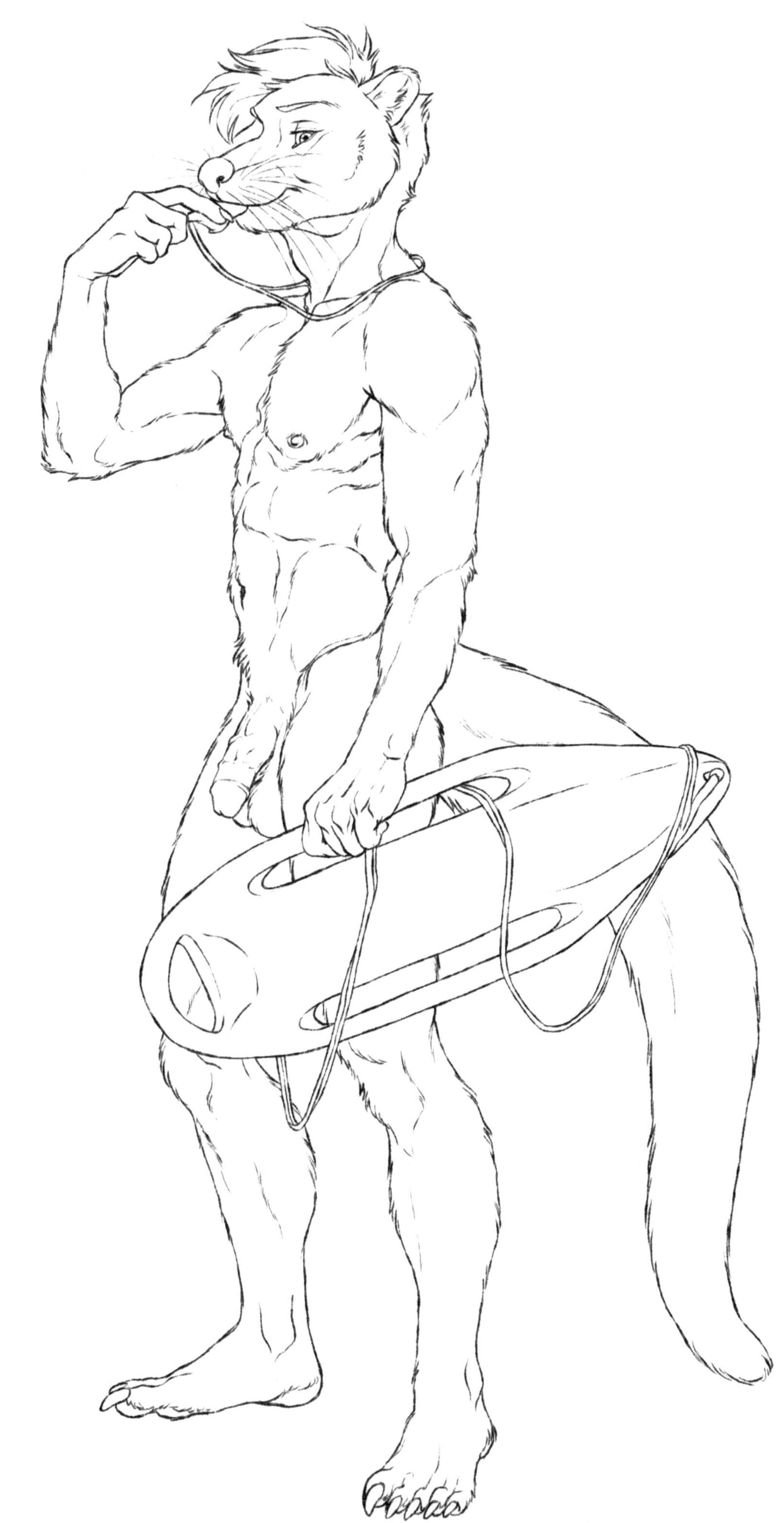

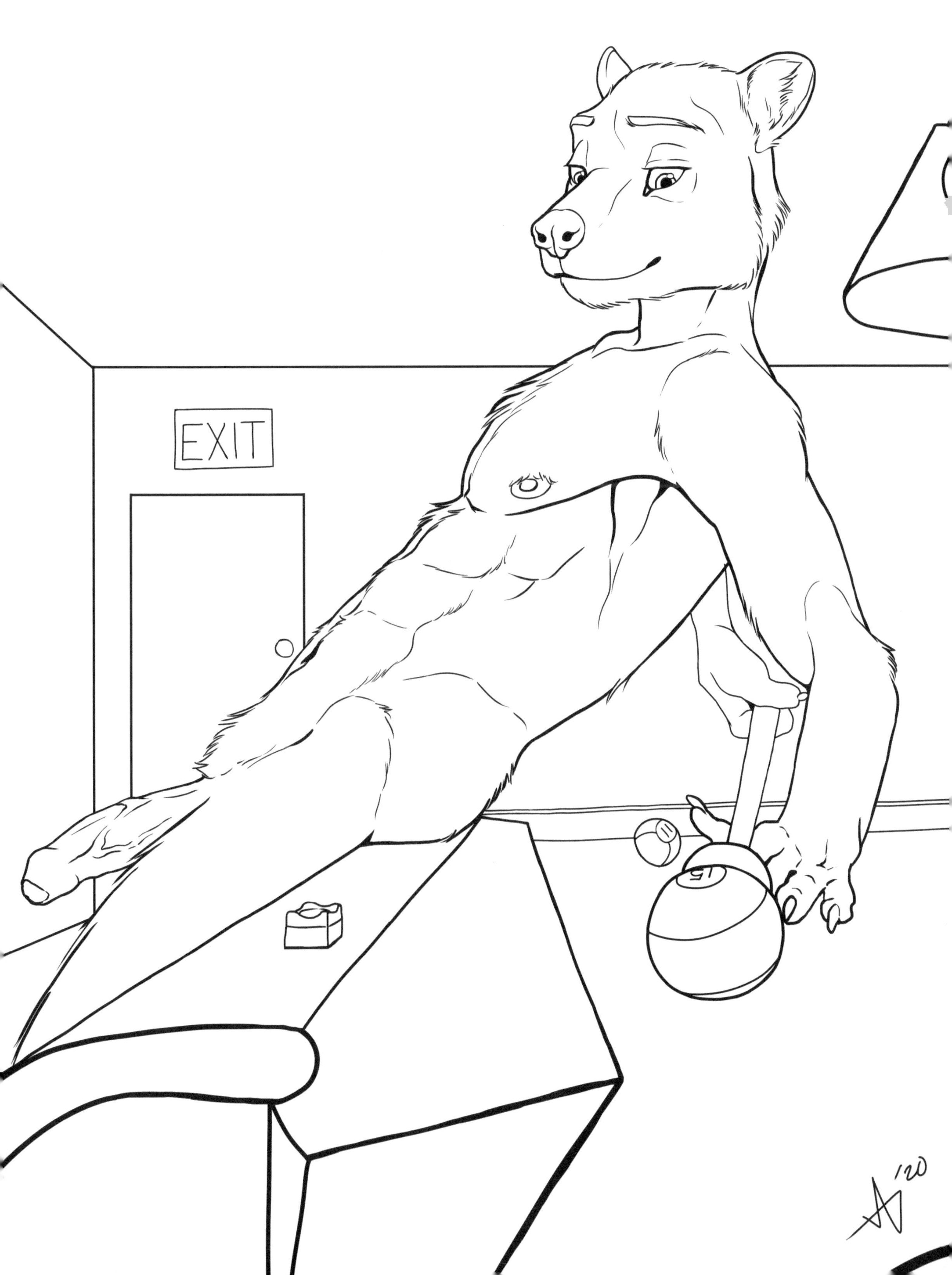
EXIT

Coors
LIGHT
TRANS
NATIONAL

www.ingramcontent.com/pod-product-compliance
Lightning Source LLC
Chambersburg PA
CBHW040830050726
47507CB00021B/167